Pod-Anim

CW00384032

(Premise)

After death technology has allowed moderately rich h
to be transported into a cybernetic body that looks ex
death seem almost obsolete. Some choose through strict privacy to choose a different body.
Either a person didn't enjoy their life, family or friends so they choose a body nothing like
their past body image but still with all their thoughts and memories intact or they choose an
exact replica of the old body if they have the money.

Of course the vocals are different but for those who choose to be in the same body image if
there is any audio of them say by video or an mp3/mp4 or answer machine message this can
be put into their new system so they're able to talk to relatives and friends as though nothing
has changed in the same pitch, tone it's seamless. Usually all the perks are afforded to the
rich who can afford and prepare for any future unforeseen circumstances namely death but
recently the criminal world have sought to profit from making pods or escaping a messy
death.

If a person was one race they can choose to come back as any other and experience it. You
have black people wanting to try the experience of being white and vice versa to see if there
are any privileges or benefits. There is always the curiosity of having what we perceive as
advantages or disadvantages associated with various races some well found some just
rumoured.

The only thing is they can't change pods once they've chosen and their family members who
felt they would see their loved ones again in the same form don't hear from them again
because they've chose a different body leaving many angered and wanting the law to change
so everyone has to disclose who they become and more importantly who they were. You can
imagine the controversy when someone choses as has happened before many times to come
back in a different body but can still interact with family or friends knowing things about
them but not disclosing their true identity.

To change Pod's now is a life sentence and many have been put away plus the only place that
has the market on pods is a large multi-million pound company called "Burls".

Characters

Samuel Hughes (main character) mid 30's black American athletic build short hair well-groomed lawyer. Backstory of facing discrimination in various forms and thus argues for anonymity because he believes racists views and discrimination will be used against people if they were of one race before and chose another and people are made aware of this.

Vanessa Hughes (Samuel's wife) uses the word "babe" when she calls Sam. Is 33 has long black hair has dimples, curvy American church goer-religious. Believes that pods are wrong and this conflicts with her faith. Before Vanessa met Samuel she was an accountant on her way to a great career she gave this up when she had her children with Samuel but she never resented him for this she always thought she'd pick it up again. Her mum Julie reminds her of her career.

Dexter Hughes (son of Sam & Vanessa) slim like his dad but without the athletic build 16. Wanting to go college

Sarah Hughes (age 8) (the daughter of Sam & Vanessa) Bushy haired, Chatty like her mother.

Leo (Sam's dad) (Deceased) used to be a big time gangster, provided for the family which was Sam and his mum but wasn't really around for them due to his criminal activities. Due to his high profile the family had to keep moving homes so they didn't get caught up in his work.

Julie (Vanessa's mum) wants what she considers the best for her daughter and that is to be earning rather than relying on Sam and end up like she did with Vanessa's father.

Kingsley (age 42) A criminal lord. Mixed-race. As a criminal wore steel capped toe boots. Uses slang a lot.

Carla (age 28) White but always tanned via creams believing sunbeds to cause wrinkles. Kingsley's girlfriend

Robert Chowe (prosecution) Chinese late 30's arrogant, rich top prosecutor in his field. "My friend" his fav quote. Tries to be humorous on many occasions.

Carlito's – rival gang to Kingsley's. Leader 40 something Italian thinning hair with an m shape at the front of his head where it is receding.

James Ryan (scientist) late 50's white balding hair in the middle has sides of his hair is like looking at a snooker table horizontally he has cushions on the side.

Anthony Burlcroft a rich tech wiz owner of Burl's.

Real life "RL" leader **Anita Kappor** (Indian) skinny activist university educated.

Luke Shaw – wants to control R.L and is more violent than Anita in his attempts to put a dent in Burl's reputation and bring them down.

Judge Douglas-married

Location and Society

North America.
I would like to tell you the world is a totally different place and that we live in peace and everything is futuristic and better but that is not the case. Imagine it's the same place you know but with man's greed for self-preservation at the expense of nature a bit more advanced in the form of these life sustaining machines/devices. No transporter beams, laser guns or food produced by a machine or flying cars.

Note to reader

Words in Italic shows a characters thoughts.
I am religious and believe in God in no way shape or form is this meant to be blasphemous by saying humans can escape death and judgement this is merely fictional in the ideas expressed and the characters formed.

Contact the author

Anchor- allusive
Instagram – allusiveebooks
Medium- Richard James
Twitter - allusiveseeker
Wordpress– allusiveebooks

If you would like to have any input in the second edition of this book in terms of what direction it can take or if you have designs for the characters appearance or location setting please send your thoughts in a message or picture on Instagram #podanimity as well as tagging me into the picture #allusiveebooks. Please note there is no payment but I can put you in the acknowledgements if you wish.

Copyright

Chapters

Chapter 1 "The Beginning or End?"

"Death normally gets the final say in all issues but not in this world or time!"

The body is on one of those metal tables that you would see at a morgue or dissecting table with four wheels rattling side to side as the medics try to be quick. Surgical instruments are shuffling in a tray on top of the body being moved. A green blanket over it, the person is dead but there's heavy security around the table as doctors rush it to a room. Five strong over fed steroids eating goons in black suits heavily armed with 9mm's keep looking over their shoulder, they know their boss Kingsley can come back from this with the help of technology and he can rule his patch as he once did. The rival gang Carlito's done their best to take him out in their last shoot out. In this world if you still have your brain and spine you can live on almost like it never happened.

It is late 22:16 to be exact the body being taken through the down town hospital is a cold slab of meat to most but this is no ordinary dead body it is a well-known criminal Kingsley. There should be no urgency but there is. The Dr's have ten hours to get the brain and spine out of the body and into a pod for the process to work, any longer than this and there's various issues of malfunctioning and rejection of tissue that can take place. A pod sounds small and cute but we are talking about a high tech piece of machinery.

The DR. wipes his sweaty brow with the back of his hand whilst working on Kingsley knowing they can't make any mistakes. The body is cut open with an electric hand saw buzzing away much like one you would cut wood with, right down the middle from the forehead down the throat, centre of the chest cracking open the breast plate and stopping just before the groin region.

Robot pincers making swift sharp sounds of precision positioning carefully the brain stem spine and all connecting nerves into the pod then like a circuit board all necessary nerve endings are connected through an adhesive substance. A jelly like fluid is used to fill the inside of the head to cushion the brain from any damage. The last part involves putting the Nano bots inside via the mouth entrance where they spread throughout the body and are being watched closely on a monitor to ensure they go to all areas.

There is also the issue of money, who wants to miss out on a pay-out for helping a wealthy criminal? Everyone with street intelligence knows there's good money to be made. The medics know there's a lot of money to be made if they keep him alive so to speak the term people use now is "Re-Born". The external or outer body is referred to by many as the "Pod". The medics risk a backlash from rival gangs for saving a perceived threat but the money makes it tempting where they can disappear to a different country or just live in anonymity in a wealthy area or of course there is the option of being Re-Born themselves but many gangsters are ensuring this doesn't happen by shooting the brain or severing the spinal column of Dr's helping rivals.

Of course Kinsley had his robot (pod) on standby with all the illegal money he made through his strip clubs that laundered drug money. It's one of the first things the rich now do, book an appointment have your face mapped on a computer, body and face measurements taken along with vocals, weight and height, eye colour all the details to make a sufficient pod replica.

Kingsley's option isn't of a replica, why come back as a well-known criminal? When you can be someone else.

To the rich it's like a life insurance that pays out with them still being alive because they feel they've cheated death, as long as they can keep the pod going. The pods simply need charging once a week which you don't forget due to system warnings during the day and night, it's not a long process it simply involves sitting down and plugging in a USB sized wire into the belly button area. Cleaning is pretty much as you would clean a human body since the technology is water proof unless you were to somehow get fully inside to all the circuits via a damaged area but any damage sustained is reported back to the company's A.I system Bertha and alerts are sent to the user. Are you sold yet do you want one?

The whole issue of knowing if a person elects to come back as someone else arose due to an instance of a man coming back in a different form that resembled someone he thought his wife was interested in and their relationship grew but he murdered her based on his jealousy when he felt she was acting more favourably to his new body then how he was treated when he was alive and a proper human. Whether this exposes our human insecurities or anger some plead the case of both but human emotions cannot be gaged at the best of times by others, who knows what makes us do what we do.

To have an exact duplicate of your former self is a lot more expensive so the average person goes for a different form due to the price or just wanting a change. To an ordinary person it is still costly, more expensive than two houses depending on the option you chose. There is option one to come back as yourself which is highly priced since the work is done before death to secure the voice, facial image and body shape, posture and other intricate parts. Option two a totally different body even race if needed the only option that isn't there for people yet is to be a different sex people have tried illegally to perform this but once found out they faced prison sentences. Why I hear you ask does it make a difference? I don't know this was the process put in place possibly because it can be seen as fraud or deception when it comes to intimacy with partners. Option three for the poorer people is a standard pod not looking as human like or with all the great features afforded to the rich but hey you've just cheated death for cheap what more do you want?

The rich pay for their pod normally but poorer people have been offered the option of paying for a pod via organ donation which many have argued causes the Dr's to favour the decision of declaring people dead more rather than trying to save their life. For a full donation of organs excluding the brain and spine necessary for the procedure poorer people can have option one. Some have found out the hard way that they had agreed, to donate all organs but woke up in a pod of a different standard because not all the organs taken from their body were useable such as alcoholics not having useful kidneys, lungs or livers.

There was a case of a man who took his Re-Born body mountain climbing in the Alps and due to conditions froze inside his pod, the cheaper option has been improved a lot since. This was before the advances that led to better temperature adjustment for the spine and brain whilst in the pod. Of course there are drawbacks for people that feel they might as well end their life to continue on as kind of an immortal in one sense because they obviously can't reproduce or enjoy the pleasures of intimacy but they can try, some would say the feeling isn't there and the women have really gone off the idea since that one incident where a woman died because of the force of a guy's pod ramming into her. You may laugh but again this was before advances made the pod more controlled in those areas and less forceful in intimacy and fights. One guy was able to punch a guy's head clean off due to the force of the arms but now custom-made upgrades aren't allowed and the force applied by pods are limited to strong but not overly forceful limits when fighting. There were instances of people arguing it was the companies fault for allowing them to punch with such force and that is not what they intended to do but due to their lack of knowledge of what their pod could do or was capable of they ended up causing serious bodily harm.

In one sense pod users have said they feel and have sensitivity with their hands and experience as a human would but you can't replicate love and the feeling in your heart of butterflies. Pod users don't need to eat they can due to an upgrade do this process to help recharge their battery and they do however need sleep for some reason due to the brain I guess not getting overloaded with constant activity.

As with everything there are limitations Dr's have around ten hours to perform the procedure of removing a spinal cord and brain from a body with any connecting nerves or veins that are of use to put inside the pod. It is intricate work but manageable when the team of neurologists, physicians and other experts know what they are doing.

Some criminals due to their activity opt to come back in a different form to try evading prison and they get away with it because of paid dodgy specialists that can triple the money they are paid for these procedures to be done without the laws knowledge and anonymity. There are a few Re-Born's in jail, those who thought they could evade capture by becoming a different person.

So that brings us to the issues facing pod users today, people wanting pod users to have their original identification (pre-death) known so they can't simply abandon an old life and start as someone else whilst knowing the people they communicate with and that person being unaware. You can imagine the drama of telling secrets to someone you think is a stranger but they had actually known you well or intimately. In the past pods were easy to identify by the appearance not looking as smooth as a human and the robotic simulated walk or robotic tinny voice but now advances mean they are very convincing as humans.

When you integrate something into society it naturally becomes part of it and accepted as normal. There have been calls for pod users to carry cards displayed on their chest showing who they were before. Many have argued this is an invasion of privacy, discrimination and a form of slavery against them so this hasn't come into force.

How the pod works with just the spine and brain alone with sometimes only minimal other nerve functions I don't know I am not a scientist but the technology exists and is being made use of. Nano technology has its part to play with the Nano bots moving around making things work is as much as I could understand from various news reports that tried to explain. Who thought of this first and patented it? is questionable but one major company Burls works on producing pods to order and create a few standard pods for poorer people based on general appearances.

There is the issue of trying not to create one pod that looks like another so the computer-generated image before the pod is developed runs a matching system to check and changes features on a pod it deems are too similar in appearance to previous pods made. There are always exceptions to who can be placed inside a pod, obviously if someone is suffering with a degenerative brain disease or disorder (Alzheimer's, Schizophrenia, Dementia or any other mental health issue) they cannot be placed inside a pod because they would still have the same problems they suffered before.

If you are in a pod before doing large investments (property, car, boat or setting up a business) you have to disclose who you were prior to death to ensure you're not a criminal and aren't trying to use funds gained through criminal activity. Each pod has a unique reference number associated with it and engraved at the back of the foot even if removed the A.I Bertha sitting in Burl's building has recognition software based on appearance and the Nano-bots used.

END

Chapter 2 "Even demons can be Re-Born"

Lying flat in his hospital bed caramel hands placed flat downwards his finger twitches
> "Ah what happened I feel like I'm drugged up my limbs are heavier, why's it taking more thought to get some motion"?
> "He's back"

Says one of his main goons Gary, smiling his allegiance pledged for what reason is unknown since his boss is one of the most ruthless towards his staff. The gang have been there all night ensuring his safety. Gary with a smirk and sinister scar across his face from an encounter as a youth instructs the others to keep a look out, they were all gathered around the hospital bed with a momentary lapse of concentration that could be costly by not ensuring their boss and surrounding area is safe from their rivals. A Dr walks in with a clipboard and pen scribbling something, all bodies turn towards him all reaching for their inside pockets or their back waist for protection, the Dr says
> "Alright you are ready to go Sir".

Kingsley responds
> "That's what I wanna hear fam let's do this"

Kingsley responds using his arms by his side to sit up in the bed, one of his goons try to help
> "Yo! Do I look like a girl to you?"

The goon lowers his head
> "No sorry boss I just"
> "Don't just nothing people have died for less don't make that mistake".

He was always one for words which can lead to deadly actions. When necessary Kingsley can be ruthless and talk like he's from the streets dressed down in jeans and a jumper but when business comes around he is a well-spoken gentleman well-groomed and suited.

A goon mentions how he can get up to all his old activities trying to lighten the mood and possibly save his mate from any further wrath from him to which Kingsley responds
> "you moron don't you know these devices are marked with a specific I.D so that people like us can't do what we want if anything this makes it harder to do anything illegal".

He's not telling them the real purpose behind his actions, he's tired of the life of looking over the shoulder all the time he's had his fill of women, money, drugs, exotic places, boats, houses. Kingsley wants to live in peace again and start fresh with possibly a family and of course the money he made.

It is going to take a day or two before Kingsley can adjust his senses and walk properly stumbling from the bed with a few steps, a green robe draped around him. Gary looks down from the hospital window clicks his fingers and says

"Get the car and bring it around back".

The goon closest to the door exits

A black 4x4 with tinted windows pulls up outside the weather is mild just a breeze no rain or distractions to worry about.

A few minutes passed again Gary looks out the hospital window of the seventh floor of fourteen

"Let's move guys keep your eyes sharp".

Kingsley has now changed into a black suit although he had pride a few minutes ago he allowed one of his men to help him change clothes they don't want to spend longer than needed.

They proceed to move down the corridors two men flanking on his left two on his right with Gary in front to take the heat if necessary, their heads on a swivel left to right the two at the back on both sides looking behind every now and then to ensure no surprises. The lift button is pressed a silver circle illuminated now by a red light appears, Gary puts his right hand in his inside blazer pocket on his left chest area to pull the heat if necessary. The elevator pings the call lift light goes off, doors open four people step out two male doctors and a woman and kid they're allowed to pass with the goons splitting sideways to allow them through they get in press the ground button and head down. Kingsley instructs them as they're going down the floors

"Look I need to look legit for a while, lay low and let the Carlito's think I'm dead".
"Sure boss no problem, what's the play?"
"I am going to go in this car and be dropped off to a location you don't know about, I need to purchase a legit property don't look for me if I need you I'll contact you".
"Boss how do we know you're ok?"
"No one knows my identity except you and those doctors for now".

Kingsley takes what he hopes is a last look at them before turning legit

"You guys have been good to me I'll see you soon until then Gary is running things"
"Boss I uh"
"You're ready Gary, do what you think I would do if you get stuck"

Gary looks over the guys seeing if they are as surprised as he is. They all seem ok no shocked expressions. Gary usually handles the lads whilst Kingsley stayed at base only showing up if a big event occurred or if needed to make a point. Through fear no one will challenge Kingsley's decision. They head towards the garage to get the car and go to Kingsley's old pad. Kingsley and a few others stay put until they bring they car closer.

Kingsley steps into the back of the 4×4 cautious of his head hitting the door frame as he goes in he still has a lot of adjustments to get used to. Placing himself gently on the leather cream seats looking at his driver he is familiar with Enrique

"You sure you're ready to do this boss?"

Enrique is one of the few to know his bosses intentions, the door closes

"Yeah it has to be done, it's time let's go"

as they drive Kingsley takes in all the scenery of downtown knowing he might not see it again for some time if he wishes to remain out the game. Corner stores selling booze, alleyways with dumpsters and fire escapes, steam vents in the roads all this stuff you don't see where Kingsley is heading. They stream past at a steady speed the last thing Enrique or Kingsley needs is unwanted attention from a traffic stop.

It is not his permanent residence just a base until he can buy a property.

     "You want a drink boss?"

Kingsley laughs

     "Is there any point?"

     "You forget what I am now? Literally a robot now"

Head facing downwards Kingsley reflects and shares his thoughts

     "I knew I'd feel like this, I have regrets Enrique, I should have done more with my life".

     "Boss don't say that I wish I could have done half the things you've done"

     "Yeah huh"

Shaking his head left to right Kingsley says looking up at the sky to his left out the window in a low tone

     "Do you know how many people I've killed? And the way I've had to do it? I've seen animals die more humanely".

Flashbacks run through his mind so vividly they sometimes visit him at night as nightmares, at times women have been ushered from his room after a rampant night of alcohol and drug fuelled sex sessions they would all be sprawled out on the bed and Kingsley would wake sweating and shouting.

     "And I respect that boss; everyone knows not to mess with you because of that"

     "It leaves mental scars Enrique not even being in this fake body can erase"

Tapping the temple of his head with one finger.

Trying to lighten the mood Enrique says

     "Alright forty minutes and we're there boss you can start fresh"

Peeping over his right hand shoulder

     "Look you're going to have to lose the boss tag otherwise people are going to ask questions"

     "No problem ... Uh what should I call you?"

     "I don't know let's say Michael for now".

Minutes later

     "Ok we are here"

They've pulled up on a nice mansion with a circular drive way that circles a green patch with an eagle statute in the middle.

     "I'll see you Enrique, thanks for all you've done remember you can't see me again I don't care what it is for. If you need me only in an emergency call"

He hands Enrique one of his guns passed to him from his goons earlier.

     "Take this it's clean no trace look after her"

He wipes it clean with a handkerchief.

     "Thanks Michael it has been a pleasure you've supported me and my family, don't know what I would have done without you".

Kingsley taps him on the right shoulder. Kingsley is still being true to himself and solid as a rock, even though saying goodbye to years of friendship. Even with intimate moments like this where he wants to say so much more he refuses to it hurts him burying feelings like this but it is necessary if his enemies knew his true feelings for some of his loyal workers they could easily exploit it by kidnapping them and demanding money or a trade of sorts.

End

Chapter 3 Samuel's back story

So many times as a young black man Sam overcame discrimination in his life to triumph, this is what drove him and made him want to be a lawyer defending people from what he could not defend himself from as a child. He still suffers flashbacks which he shares with his wife Vanessa whilst in bed on the first floor of their home.

"When I was a kid I remember being told by a white friend as we approached his house, there's this boy and he doesn't like people of other races so when people go past his house he fires ball bearing pellets at them"

"I found this hard to believe but we walked past an open window which my friend had mentioned and heard a noise hit a door to the right of us"

"I didn't see or feel anything but he began to run and said run"

"I couldn't comprehend at the time why someone simply based on a different race would want to harm me or what gave them the right to feel they could harm me?"

For all Sam's dad's reputation he couldn't get respect from these guys that looked down on him because of his race, most didn't know about his dad because to them they were concerned with criminals of their race that governed their areas and Sam's dad only dealt with black areas until the times and people changed. Growing up with suspicious activity was what Samuel knew and learnt from his dad this is that made him different and what he is today, trying to be the exact opposite of what he observed. Although his father had respect, money a reputation and a high profile Sam wanted to do things legitimately and not have to watch over his shoulder. Too often as a youngster Sam had to move homes with his parents and sometimes without his dad's presence. This was to ensure other rival gangs don't know his family's location. The best way to bring someone down from their perch is to use leverage in this case family members so Sam's dad always did the upmost to shield Sam his mother and sister from imminent danger. Sometimes hard drugs were stored in the house but never near where Sam could gain access, such as coke stored in the inside of the washing machine where the stone weight sits making it hard for police or sniffer dogs to detect. Sometimes inside the car in small amounts within the car horn at the centre of the steering wheel.

Of all the things Sam had witnessed his dad do he could never pin-point anything specific to say he was a bad guy he had always been shielded from seeing violence or drug deals that his father was involved in but he did know of them and hear through rivals, school and his dad's own employees the extent of his dad's actions. It did give Sam the education he needed and stability of wealth that his dad taught him should be earned not inherited.

In many bad situations, times and errors in Sam's life he could of placed the blame on his dad's actions but in the end Sam believed we are all responsible for our own lives when we reach a certain age and it is counterproductive to blame others when you have gained from them in one way or another.

Getting into university was easy due to his father's wealth and connections but gaining genuine friends and people that cared was harder, this is why when Vanessa came along and knew nothing of his father they became close and it benefited him making him see a potential future with her rather than the women that would be with him to either please his father or gain from saying they had been with the lucrative son and benefit from a posh meal or hotel for the night.

Chapter 4 "the United Family"

The Hughes' are at home sitting around a white surfaced breakfast bar the sun glistening off its marble top. Samuel is reading out his case to his wife Vanessa who's getting breakfast ready for her and the kids, taking out the plates from the cabinets gently. She's not happy

"What do you mean? You're going to fight for this creep?"

"Vee, I just need you to understand you know I always been for people's privacy and non-discrimination".

Vee is his pet name for her, or backup word when he needs her on board.

"Yeah non-discrimination is fine but you are deliberately and knowingly defending a big time criminal".

Her voice goes to a higher pitch when irate.

Vanessa takes off her ring to wash the dishes Samuel complains that it isn't going to be affected by water or scrapes

"It's an expensive ring Vee a little water and scrape isn't going to make the diamond fall off"

she corrects him

"Diamond? You mean my main diamond babe surrounded by three beautiful mini-diamonds ha-ha"

This was the ring she always wanted and Samuel had bought it for her. Vanessa always got upbeat when talking about her ring it meant so much to her to have the man of her dreams. Sam knew this little reminder would be a soother to quieten the tension.

Samuels's mobile rings with its standard built in ringtone, the display says Kingsley, all his clients numbers he liked to input as soon as he had details of a case. Of course this was a client he had to keep secret except for his family members being told.

he pulls it out his right pocket looking down at the screen before placing it to his ear.

"Hello, I hear you've been assigned my case and I hear good things about you"

"How did you get my…?"

"Don't worry, you know who I am?"

"Yes of course I need to know my client in order to take the case"

"Then you know I have ways to get information, but look I know it's early but 12pm Joes dinner we need to discuss a few things"

Click the call ends. Samuel knows who he is dealing with and knows he's not the kind of person to give alternates to, if Kingsley states something you just do it! Within reason of course! Discussing with Vanessa you could hear the frustration, Sam questions

"Why Joe's? It's not exactly private!"

Still floating around the kitchen preparing breakfast, Vee's voice is high pitched again but this time in humour

"Well at least you know you'll be safe he's not going to harm you in public".

"Oh thanks hun that's just what I need to hear".

Sam gathers his files together shuffling them in a hurry in his brown leather briefcase, Vanessa fixes his black and grey stripped tie gives him a peck on the lips and says she'll be going church. They still maintain their affection even over the years and with all the changes. In some scenarios they are ying and yang which makes some couples get along, Vee is tidy and neat Sam often scruffy but she'd normally clean up after him or correct his dress sense.

Church is her normal sanctuary to pray for family needs. Sam knows he's in trouble, when she goes to pray over issues she normally wins.

She's also going to pray for cramps that have been in her belly and back she's been getting that she's seen the DR for and waiting for the x-ray and blood results.

As Sam is leaving Vee mentions they haven't seen "Uncle Eddie" for a long time he is not actually Sam or Vanessa's brother but has been a lifelong friend of Sam, helping him through thick and thin. When they were young and even when older Sam never used his family name or dad (Leo) to scare people off or gain anything but if Eddie was around he would be the one to whisper in the ear of whoever was trying to trouble Sam not to mess with him because of his dad which would cause the trouble maker to go away sheepishly. Eddie would never make it obvious to Sam what he was doing to ward off trouble neither did he want to tell too many people just in case the wrong person found out. Sam used to greet Eddie with a handshake and hug often Ed would come around for breakfast also he often baby sat the kids when they were younger. Ed was one of the few men Sam could trust around Vee and the kids whether he was home or not, the sad thing is Ed never really had his own life in terms of a kid or wife but was one of those serial daters you could tell was searching for the one but just couldn't find her. Often, he would praise Sam and Vee and talk of his admiration and wishing that he could have half of their happiness.

Sam heads off in his red Vauxhall before even saying bye to the kids who are off school for the holidays. He has a lot on his mind what with Vanessa waiting to hear from the Dr's and this case. Running it over in his mind what to argue on behalf of his client and what Kingsley could want such an informal meeting for?

The kids come down the stairs hands sliding against the rail Dexter first slim like his dad but without the athletic build, 16 and wanting to go to college possibly follow in dad's footsteps studying law. Sarah comes down bushy haired, chubby like her mother and chatty. They sit to eat breakfast that is now out and ready, pancakes with a selection of sauces and fruit. Vanessa always says to the family you have to balance out the bad with the good. She has been trying to eat healthy since getting stomach cramps over the last few months, ignoring them to fulfil her motherly and wife duties that she always valued after seeing her mum and dad's poor example of a relationship and parenting.

They discuss what they thought was an argument
　　　"Mum what are you guys arguing about now?"
Says Dexter after shovelling in a piece of pancake into his mouth
　　　"No argument honey just me and your dad discussing his new case, you know he
　　　loves fighting against injustice and discrimination"
　　　"Oh yeah tell me about it"
Sarah says whilst hitting Dexter in his shoulder for putting another pancake on his plate taken from the stack in the middle. Dexter's a fast eater with a fast metabolism that keeps him slim.
　　　"Oi! You guys stop that, you know your dad getting involved from the start trying to
　　　protect people before knowing the full case".
Vanessa explains what she knows to the kids. Dexter is panicked upon hearing the name of his dad's client even though he was eavesdropping a bit
　　　"Mum you know who this guy is? He's dangerous"
　　　"Yeah I know Hun but that's why I advised caution but your dad has gone to see him
　　　now".
　　　"Don't worry I am going church now I'll say a prayer for him".

Vanessa was going to pray for him regardless of the case this is her partner that had been through so much with her and had given her a good time last night, which is what had a small sinister smirk come across her face highlighting her dimples.

<u>END</u>

Chapter 5 the Meet and Greet

Samuel meets Kingsley's stare as he walks from his car to the diner
Can't stare too long this guy can snap at any minute
They can see each other through the glass window showing the upper half of people's bodies, the drive wasn't long. Kingsley's sitting in a booth with a table in the middle and bench on each side to fit about four to five people but there isn't four people just him. The diner theme is a red, silver metallic 60's look with stools that are a pole from the ground with a red circle leather top for a seat.

He has ordered already, a burger fries and shake. Many would wonder what is the point of a pod eating? With technology the food is broken down to produce electric so the pod doesn't need to charge via the usb and it's a force of habit for some scientists are yet to establish if it is a psychological element that means you still seek food or down to the individual.
Eating is also a way to socialise and a way of people perceiving a pod user as a human without realising what they really are.

With a mouth full he speaks after hearing Samuel walk in with the bells jingling above Joe's entrance door.
> "Mmmnnn grab yourself a seat sorry I couldn't wait I was hungry or should I say curious, order what you want it's on me".

Sam is more curious than hungry
> "You came alone?"
> "Yeah why? Who do you want to see? I'm your client"

He must be confident no one knows his identity and even if they did he is somewhat untouchable.

Kingsley tells him how he wants to make a new life for himself now that he has a pod and only a few know of his previous life but the circumstances surrounding his death with his gang around him meant it is not as easy as he planned he couldn't come back anonymously because members of his gang saw the pod he was placed in and thus know his identity.

> "That's not the life I pictured when I was kid robbing, stealing, killing I had dreams I had ambition".

He breaks down crying or at least a pods simulation of crying, it's not what Sam expected.
Does he have a heart after all? or is this a game by a calculated killer
> "I put off having kids I didn't want them to see daddy a criminal".

Now as a pod Kingsley knows he can't realise his dream of having kids but can still get out of the criminal world with the help of Samuel firstly by winning his case.
> "Look at me"

Banging the palm of his hand against the side of his head where the temple is situated producing a metallic sound through the rubber like material over the outside.

Time has passed Samuel and Kingsley argue over if the jury find out his past and who he is, it would leave him with no chance of winning his case. Samuel mentions they can compel evidence in the pre-trial so they know the evidence that will be used against them.

"That's why I've been hearing so much about you, you know your stuff".
This is Sam's bread and butter nothing hard about this. Sam receives a pat on his right shoulder blade from Kingsley's right hand as Kingsley has put down a $50 to cover a $50 meal and got up to now leave. Sam wants to fight for the small guy in this case the waitress and her tip, he never knew who to pick a fight with and who to leave alone his reactions for these incidents were too fast

"Um did you forget to leave a tip?"
"No they should be grateful I ate here"
Swinging his body back around to now face Sam
"Do you know the kind of meals I eat and I'm eating this crap!"
Lifting a plate on another table with one finger as if to diminish its quality whilst Sam assesses that Kingsley's plate was clean with no pieces of food left behind so it couldn't have been that bad, if pods actually taste and enjoy their food, so he responds

"But the service deserves a tip these people work hard for minimum reward"
"And whose fault is that?" "They should get a better job"
Reaching to his back pocket of his smooth black trousers Kingsley takes out his wallet Sam is relieved he thought he could of easily have pulled a gun or knife. Walking back towards the table he drops a $20 on top of the $50 left

"Is that enough for you?"
Wiping his wing tipped shoe with his finger which is now elevated on the leather seat where he was sitting with his fingers. Sam reassess the situation Kingsley dressed smart with his smooth appearance and obvious abundance of money.
Before he leaves he turns to Sam

"I am glad we're on the same page say hi to Vanessa for me".
Everything was ok up until that point Sam knew Kingsley could get information on him but what did he know about Vanessa or the kids?
What did it all mean a top criminal who could have chosen anyone from a list of high profile lawyers, but he chooses an upcoming lawyer? Was it his stance or passion in trials?
Left confused Sam mulls it over and contemplates whether Vee and the kids should know how things went and the fear of challenging him about the tip.
Sam had only received vital information of Kingsley after accepting the case otherwise he might not have taken it. Sometimes too much attention can be bad and this was likely to get a lot of attention from the media not to mention protest groups.

END

Chapter 6 "Respect me, respect my family"

Kingsley's gang has no name unlike the Carlito's there was no need! People just knew of Kingsley and his territory and once you obeyed the rules you were ok. Namely don't interfere with his gangs business or gang members and you'll be fine.

They were viewed as one of the gangs that were justified in their actions and did not kill innocent people just rivals that deserved it. Not one of Kingsley's members were reckless because if they were they had to answer to him, as far as he was concerned you represent him and Kingsley wanted respect from people not fear and that is what he got, respect.

Sam viewed and liked Kingsley mostly because what he saw in Kingsley was a reflection of his dad a guy who you knew had values and was good at his core but did bad to look after his family and others, the only way he knew how. Although there was a sense of resentment for his dad because of the changes he had to make in order to escape his father's rivals he understood that this couldn't be perceived by his father at the time, his father was still old fashioned in his ways and not up to date with technology. Due to his dad's ignorance and lack of understanding when his time was up he accepted death like the man he was and didn't consider pods that was relatively new at the time. Sam often thought how things could be different if he was alive still, would Sam have bothered to continue in law or could he? after having his father go from a well-known local gangster to a public gangster due to the Carlito's exposure of him to the media.

END

Chapter 7 "Like father like son"

Dexter wants to pursue a career like his father because this draws him nearer to his father and gives them something in common. Dexter often hears of the disconnect between his father Sam and Sam's father Leo through his mother and feels his dad wants more of a close knit relationship.

Sam often thought he was a disappointment to his dad who would have loved nothing more than his son taking over his well-run empire. Some people are born into it and take to the criminal world like a duck to water and some don't.
He can always see his dad's face light up when he talks of fighting for the less able or marginalised. Dexter has never been the sport type to watch games with his father or play in them.

Dexter is talking with his dad who has come to his bedroom to check on him and is keeping his safe distance by the door entrance holding the door frame one hand on each side like they were going to close. According to his mum and dad the distance is necessary to avoid the odour of a young teenager who spends most of his time in his room.
> "Dad, mum told us about the case. I understand the personal reasons why you took it"
> "Before pods came along I don't know what we would have done dad you know after you..."

Sam stops him mid-sentence never wanting to focus on negative past events
> "Erm let's not mention that around the house son remember your sister is still too young to remember and understand, you know how sensitive she is".
> "Yeah just saying it would have been hard to cope I can't see how mum is so against pods yet look at the benefits?"
> "You know your mum can be stubborn for a while"

After hearing that Dexter knew his dad was telling the truth and that he has his profession and actions for justice, through a respect for his own fortune and that of others.

Sam thought to himself the respect Dexter has for him is much like that he had for his own father but hopefully without the feeling of guilt along with knowing they do bad to benefit the family whereas Sam had tried to lead a straight life clean of any of his father's associations.

End

Chapter 8 "Resistance is futile"

Reallife are an underground group based in a warehouse, hiding out due to one of their many actions such as robbing a truck full of pods and setting fire to it even stealing bodies that were prepped to go for re-birth. They believe the dead should accept their fate or karma and not try cheat death they use the stolen pods for parts and to fund their activities.

The group numbers fifty maximum but with support in the public, they claim pods are no way for society to live and it interrupts the natural order with a population decreasing less and consuming more. As a youngster living forever seemed cool, you get to see advances in technology and never lose a loved one. When is enough, enough? When do you say you've seen all you can and don't want to see any more pain and suffering and the cruelty of man towards each over and the planet. What about if your kids or grandkids decide they don't want to be re-born and you out live most of your family?

There is less of a burden on the health system due to the minimal upkeep and maintenance carried out at Burls. Pod users don't seek a DR. or hospital they need to go to Burls the main company for producing pods and its associated technology.
There are many Burl sites to cope with demand. Pods rarely go wrong.

The R.L leader an Indian born woman, Anita Kapoor, University educated but resents mankind's grip and shaping of people's destiny. The resistance has made a virus to spread from Nano-bots from Bertha (the main A.I in Burls) and back to the Nano –bots they have tried before but haven't been able to perfect the technology. Not actually attempting to infect Bertha but they have set up a system to simulate the effects of the virus on an A.I system.

The choice of gender, modified eye colour, removal of genetic defects this exists and is in use but for humans not pod owners. Anita believes all God's work shouldn't be tampered with. Obviously not all people can cheat death only the rich people who may have saved a bit or organ donors but that still leaves a larger population than there would normally be if they died naturally and companies are always trying to accommodate the less wealthy.

Anita discusses with the group ways to shut down the pods. Their best chance is the virus there's been no other suggestions that seem feasible; manually there are thousands of pods it would take the reliance on individual citizens globally being brave enough to find pod users and take action effectively killing someone in their pod. Many argue they aren't alive anyway as a brain and spinal cord they had died a long time ago. Many question do they have a spirit and soul still?

"Look we won't get another chance at this we have to get it right first time around" The group is gathered around in a circle with Anita perched in the middle on a stool hands clasped on the front between her legs.

Many secretly back the movement online by social media claiming their actions are sometimes justified. Others claim violence can never achieve peace. Anita in her podcasts always states to her followers without the violence and disorder their cause would be ignored.

The group survive by donations made directly sometimes and indirectly at others with every attack they have been more secluded and underground due to the governments clamping down on them and lack of evidence in most situations.

Luke (regarded as second in command) interrupts the groups' discussions

"I say Burl's isn't that well-guarded it's more hi-tech to keep people away from Bertha but with the right weaponry we should be able to get to her".

Anita comes back with rationale

"My source on the inside tells me even with force any inflicted damage in machinery there and Bertha is smart enough to know and alert the police and as far as I know this isn't a kamikaze mission".

Luke now leaves the circle to walk in the middle near Anita

"If I had ten to fifteen individuals willing to take a risk with me"

Looking around the circle for support, it's a confident look because he knows there are others that like him get frustrated with their efforts so far. Anita speaks on behalf of the group

"What exactly is your plan Luke? If it's clear and you have the support you need you can go"

Gesturing with her hand open palm facing upwards

"But where does that leave the rest of us if you fail?"

Pointing and spinning around pointing with her finger like a clock hand

"Burls will be more alert than ever to a threat with even more protection".

Luke responds

"well with your permission I want some of the best weapons we have at our disposal explosives, shotguns, assault rifles, AK47'S, night vision goggles and more we have a floor plan thanks to your connect and we'll proceed as fast as possible to Bertha and blow her up"

Punching his fist in the air, most of the group laugh knowing that AI such as Bertha is not confined to one machine but moves through the cloud, Wi-Fi and other means. In one sense this freedom of movement is best for the AI's protection but in another that increases its vulnerability. Luke's face has changed to a harsher frowned appearance, the group realises and the laughter is short lived. Anita without trying to embarrass but educate says

"That would be good Luke but this AI is well beyond being confined to one machine" Luke goes back to his seat".

Anita pulls out a piece of paper from her back pocket and changes the subject slightly

"I don't know who exactly monitors or is regulating Bertha but we have seen her level of intelligence increase and this begs the question is that through man's help or is she doing this herself and if she is doing this herself, why?" Is there any regulations on her learning?

Most of the group responds unanimously with a

"Yeah"

And hum agreement.

Members take it in turns to voice concerns a female says

"What need does AI have for humans once it can function by itself? Will a few humans be kept as slaves for maintenance of the machines?"

A man then states

"Who's going to pay a human? When AI just needs electric and can work around the clock"
Another man
"AI is not involved in the military yet as far as we are aware! But what happens when they do control planes or weapons? and decides to turn them on humans"
The group had often discussed many more theories:

- What if there is a world of pod users alone they may live forever but without children. Do they have real feelings or emotions and when do they cease being human? How far does the technology go into them and their mind?

- Is there a need for procreation and births if there is a population that's not going to die?
- Since A.I revolves around solving problems they question whether A.I will try to solve mankind's big issues such as war famine and death and is that solution for or against mankind's interest

End

Chapter 9 Everybody needs somebody

In walks Carla with her knee high black suede boots, Kingsley's prized possession regardless of the many women he'd been with Carla was what he wanted at the end of it all. She kept him grounded at times and understood his lust for women drink and violence. She understood as in tolerated him being with them for a night or two but as long as there was never any true feelings she could understand a man's lust as she had these lusts of her own but always stayed faithful to Kingsley, whether through respect or fear. Some think she endured this due to his wealth that allowed her to buy the finest clothes, cars and look after her family but who knows? She took care of her mother and two sisters herself and Kingsley never got around to having kids due to the nature of Kingsley's work it wouldn't be ideal.

Kingsley enters through the double wooden doors pushing them both open at the same time looking up towards stairs arching up on the left and right towards a wooden banister.
"Hey daddy is that you?"
As she looks down from the banister her long tanned legs are showing above her boots and a full cleavage are on display she was younger than Kingsley by a good ten years. She was respected by the gang for her ability to stop Kingsley from going too far with his violence and the fact that a gang member lost an eye when starring too long for Kingsley's liking and trying to justify it. It was a sad sight for anyone there watching even they winced and grimaced slightly.
This was a few years ago in one of Kingsley's other bases of operation
"Dolph I've seen you watch Carla like she was a piece of meat I don't like it, don't let me tell you again"
"Sorry boss, but you have to admit she's a beautiful lady I just wanted to give her that respect by making sure she knows"
Kingsley pivoted like he was going to make a basketball shot to his left at the same time he had removed a Parker pen from his front blazer pocket pressed the button down so the point was out and with his fist gripping it slammed it into Dolph's eye.

"Who the fuck are you mate? To be looking at my woman and trying to justify it to
me are you mad?"
Dolph had dropped down to his knees quickly grabbing the pen and his eye with both hands
screaming in pain apologising you can only assume to preserve his life. Kingsley had walked
over to his desk to get his 9mm that was there placing his hand on it to pick it up Carla placed
her hand on his and told him
"No please he's not worth it"
One hand on his inside leg to get his attention onto other things.
He settled walked over to Dolph calmly and toe punted him in the belly, Dolph's in a bent
over pile on the floor holding his belly with one hand and his eye with the next. For all
Kingsley's wrong he did have a heart and provided for Dolph's family since he was deemed
no longer fit for work, it was a small gesture considering he caused the problem and it could
have been so much worse.
Her flashback is over she runs down the stairs to embrace him
"Oh you feel real still"
With a sense of surprise in her voice
"Thanks babe"
Giving her a kiss on her lips
"So, does this operate still?"
Grabbing him below his waist with a firm hand.
"I've been told it does to an extent but I can't imagine it's the same as if I were real,
not for me anyway, you might enjoy it or already be used to it with all your gadgets"
They laugh as she whispers in his ear
"You are a real boy Pinocchio now lie to me and make it grow"
It is things like this that he loved about her, not too rude but just enough. They both burst out
laughing
"Let me give you a tour daddy"
"Have you settled in ok?"
"Yeah, the only thing missing was you"
Leading him by the hand around and telling him all the features and what she bought to
improve the place.

End

Chapter 10 "I know you!"

Kingsley is holding a meeting alone with one individual trying to assess his financial position
after explaining the exact amount he needs cleaned and made to look legit
"Can you make this happen?"
He asks, a female voice responds
"Yes no problem I just need assurances"
"No problem we've got everything in place, the pod for your husband is ready as soon
as we see you've done your part it will be available"
"Good, I'm sure he'll need it soon based on the way he's going"
Rubbing her forehead with her palm
"Yes I've been watching him with interest"
Kingsley calls Gary in
"Gary, where's that cheque?"
Gary comes through the door reaching into his inside pocket to retrieve the cheque.

Kingsley explains the terms to make it absolutely clear, pacing back and forth with his head down contemplating

"After your work for us is done we will let you know of more work but remember we don't negotiate on our privacy, you try blackmailing us and you know I don't like to threaten ladies but let's just say you love Sam and want to spend a long time with him".

"I understand, I just need the money and that's all I don't want any more involvement".

Kingsley with a palm now across his face sliding it down from his forehead to his mouth

"we tell you when you've finished working for us"

Chuckling almost to himself

"it's a lot of money we're giving you and we are not asking much in return, just play with numbers make everything look like it's from a legit business source and where it goes"

"I know thanks"

Vanessa scrambles up out of the leather swivel chair not wanting to annoy him anymore. On approaching the door to leave turns to say

"I'll call you when I've finished the first set of transactions"

Gary who is standing by the door hands her the cheque she takes it and folds it placing it in her purse

"The rest will be paid in cash and delivered by one of my guys".

"So that's one area covered what about my second back-up idea we discussed?"

"That is a lot easier to do, when you feel the time is right let me know and we can make it happen"

"You know I am not really sure about it yet I've never been for the idea, it's just a consideration depending on how things go with Sam"

"of course say no more"

The door closes Kingsley and Gary talk

"So Leo's boy might need a pod soon? Based on daddy's bad behaviour, interesting. "How's our lawyer boy progressing?"

Gary gives him an update.

END

Chapter 11 Leo the Lionheart

Have you ever met a "criminal" that took care of his community? Well with Leo you were safe in your area you could walk around, no one would rob you or commit acts of violence because Leo and his men had established, they won't stand for it! Leo's men took action immediately upon hearing of any grievances and got the job done to ensure people felt safe.

People could earn their way through honest work and try to do better for themselves and family, the area had community spirit. Leo established after school clubs for kids gave out food for Christmas to the poorer individuals and families and ensured businesses were not being hustled for payoffs from criminals that wanted to extort protection money. Leo never sought his money off the ordinary man or woman he took on the criminals of this world.

All his actions earned him respect for him and his crew if you ask the locals they wouldn't want anything to change when you compare other areas that had a crime lord over them that would profit from them and do what they wanted with their business such as claim free meals and drinks, Leo and his gang would pay their way and tip generously. The only fear he wanted to establish was the fear of the people in his absence if you tried to make a decent living and provided a service for the community you were valued.

END

Chapter 12 "Church not just on Sunday's"

Vanessa finds a spot to park with the family's second car an old run about, purchased when times were even better for the Hughes' Vanessa had her high-flying accountant job which she loved and thrived in which according to her mum she threw away to be with Samuel and raise kids. There is still a tone of resentment to this day when Vanessa's mum Julie speaks to Samuel. Julie used to enjoy her retirement and the money Vanessa provided to help her travel around the world almost like a bucket list. After Vanessa gave her job up that extra income dried up. Julie is one of those parents who constantly remind their children of the sacrifice they went through for them.

"What happens when Sam no longer wants or needs you?"

Is the constant reminder, Vanessa knows this is the fear and resentment her own mother holds towards her father when he left the family. She always accused her husband of cheating she wasn't the most positive of individuals but she grew up an old-fashioned woman where women were women and men were men. Women cooked cleaned maintained the house men went and earned as a provider and if there were kids the women stayed at home.

Walking in to the side entrance she admires the usual coloured glass windows with the light reflecting in that makes a nice effect on the solid concrete floors. She is there on time for a confession that she does every week to exhume herself. She knocks the wooden door one of three that says confession she can tell it's vacant because there are signs like that in a shop front that you turn to say busy or vacant instead of open and closed. She isn't concerned with which priest she tells her sins to just the advice she gets and the acknowledgement that she will be forgiven. She begins by kneeling on the small padded cushion placed on the floor in front of the wooden mesh design that you speak through, it can't be called a room it has the feel of a booth. Crossing herself with her right hand and then clasping her hand together she begins

"Father I ask forgiveness in the name of our Lord and Saviour Jesus Christ"

"Proceed child there is always forgiveness when sins are confessed and forgiveness and repentance is sought"

She can tell by the voice it is father Matthew

"I face the same continuing battle Father, my greed and longing to work again and be successful but at the expense of not looking after my family"

Her thoughts run over her mum continuously asking her when she's going back to her accounting job, it used to make Julie proud to tell people of her daughter the accountant

"We can all only do our best, have you sought an answer from the Lord in prayer?"

"Yes I have but am yet to see what he wants from me"

"He will guide you when the time is right; everything works towards his timing as long as you release your faith"

"That is another problem Father, I am finding my faith tested as I have had stomach cramps for a while now and don't know why"

Reaching to her stomach and rubbing it in a circular motion as if the priest could see.

"Have you sought help from the professionals yet? And prayed?"

"Yes Father I am awaiting the results"

"Ok then I will pray with you"

Reaching for the bible left in each booth he guides her to the right scripture and they both read out the verses. Upon thanking the father and exiting the booth she goes to kneel in the isle and say a pray before leaving and heading home.

On the way home Vanessa's mother calls with the usual preface of asking how things are and seeming happy before diving into her real issue over the car speaker system

"So how was church dear?"

"Good mum how are you?"

Trying to deflect from the inevitable

"Good you know me not doing much in my retirement just TV and gardening"

"How's the apple tree?"

"It's there ready to bear fruit soon, so how are the kids and Sam?"

With enthusiasm

"They're good; Sam's got a really big case"

Trying to pass on the enthusiasm to her mum with little success. Anyone externally would question whether her mother was actually jealous of what she had with Sam and didn't actually want her daughter to have a successful marriage because she couldn't maintain one herself.

END

Chapter 13 A.I at the Company Burls

The company headquarters of Burls is situated in the rich part of town with the coffee, luxury bags and expensive cars parked all around on top of a small hill sits the latest tech and security. It is one of those areas where the rich park anywhere with their cars and can pay a fine for parking there to them it is like putting a few pounds in a metre like an ordinary person would.

Owned by Anthony Burlcroft a rich tech wiz who like Steve Jobs got people to do what he couldn't do, or was not good at for a price. He simply had the right idea at the right time after seeing his dad die having his life support machine switched of.

He always thought there was a way to preserve him and pod's is what he came up with the life support for the pre/post-dead if that's the correct way to think of it.

Anthony's father had a traffic accident and was left paralyzed on life support but Dr's stated there was no hope for him to move or communicate again so suggested they switch off the machine. Neither Anthony a young man of fifteen or his mum could afford to keep it on at the time.

A lot of people had sympathy for Anthony due to his dad's death but many questioned his ethics even comparing him to the creator of the monster in Frankenstein arguing the religious view point of whether it is in God's plans for people to cheat death when their natural life has finished and whether they should just accept death and go on to be judged and live in the eternal spiritual world. If you by pass death then it's like there is no judgement. There is also the ethical/moral view of whether your loved ones should have to cope with a person either choosing to come back as themselves which is hard to come to terms with seeing a person resemble a real human but in reality are just components or someone choosing to look and be someone else which can often upset a family that is waiting for the person to come back and say hello like nothing happened.

A.I and Nano-bots working together was Burl's secret weapon unknown to the public until recently this was never questioned.

People did wonder how his firm is more advanced than others having a monopoly on pods in a sense; it seems other companies can't get certain aspects to work successfully. Many point to the help of advanced A.I. that can calculate and work through problems a lot faster than a human thus providing solutions and calculating risk factors.

The A.I named Bertha creates new faces to be used for pods just like police facial recognition systems it runs a process to ensure no duplicate faces are made. Orders are made in accordance with a death of someone that pre-applied. Celebrities have died and the public have demanded they be brought back but without the person's consent prior to death this won't happen even families have tried to claim it is in their best interest and this has been rejected by the courts. In the past machines with such capabilities were the size of rooms but Bertha is the size of a fridge with so much processing capability drawing information from as many reliable sources as it can. The one limitation that is established for all A.I in law is that they cannot have free access to communicate with each other as to ward off any threats of them developing ideas against humanity or their own language, it is for humans to know at all times the limitations of them and their expansion.

James Ryan a well-regarded scientist worldwide discovers that in his part of Africa where his lab is, there is no Wi-Fi just land access to the internet hence the lack of control of Nano-bots this is why when a pod travels to this part of Africa their body malfunctions and the pod owner seeks help back in America where they take a sample of the Nano-bots to discover why they stopped receiving Wi-Fi updates that are emitted in America and other parts of the world and thus didn't work properly. They could only carry out basic tasks that were pre-programmed but not adjust to other requirements placed on the body due to a lack of updated information. It is a continuous learning process for the Nano-bots to adjust to the demands of a human body in different circumstances.

During this period of malfunctions the person questioned why they didn't look like themselves and wanted to view the contract they signed. They go to Burl's to discover they had originally signed a contract to be in a pod resembling his old body but at the last minute when the Nano-bots were activated days before his fore-known death he changed his mind and signed a new contract but the old contract had been deleted in Bertha's main system and was found in the old system logs after much searching. Sometimes as part of the nano-bots process of understanding the individual the bots enter the human before death to understand and pick up familiar habits and movements, phrases, memories and then are removed to sit and wait at Burls sometimes for a long time until the persons death sometimes not so long.

END

Chapter 14 "Hospital food yum, yum"

Sam is at home managing the kids, something he's not accustomed to but manages every now and then.

The call came during the day Vanessa had to get to the hospital A.S.A.P her first thoughts are Sam and the kids but she's a woman of faith so can deal with anything, she tells herself.
    "Mr's Hughes?"

"Yes"

"This is Gatefield general hospital we have the results of your blood test and MRI and we'd like you to come in with an overnight bag please"

"How long would I need to be there?"

"Probably a few days".

"We can tell you more upon arrival, it's better in person".

She knows it can only be bad otherwise they could discuss it over the phone.

She gets her things together and leaves for the hospital.

END

Chapter 15 Trial day

The law has slightly changed with the Identity Cards Act possession of false identification for the purpose of passing off oneself as another or improperly obtaining a benefit or enrichment for yourself or others. The maximum penalty is ten years imprisonment the minimum is a $1,000 fine. For it to be a minimum penalty you have to have been doing something minor like a driving i.d fraud or seeking to obtain alcohol but for property purchases it is the maximum.

Culpability is based on:
1. Clear knowledge of the false documents
2. Is it more than one person seeking to gain?
3. Impact on others
4. Planned or pre-meditated. Evidence of planning is shown through documents whereas pre-meditation is often caught through witness statements.

Mitigating circumstances
1. Minor part in the role
   In this case Kingsley used his pod I.D so wasn't actually lying but didn't disclose as law requires his pod I.D along with his past I.D
2. Genuine remorse
3. Admission
4. Cooperation with authorities

Pre-trial

The Pre-trial is taking place in which documents are filed before the case so no surprise evidence is submitted and the other party can prepare and ask for things to be excluded or included. Being held in a side room within the court building the judge sits there with an air of authority his hands clasped resting on the table in front of him his silver wedding band reflecting the light. Samuel and Robert stand before him to make their pleas for the inclusion and exclusion of evidence and to ensure no surprises. Sam knows how Robert can be a comedian inside and out of court.

Samuel is arguing for the suppression of evidence against his client Kingsley stating

"Using my client's past to show him as a ruthless drug lord will prejudice the jury in many ways"

Robert interrupts

"And why not let the jury know who they are dealing with?"

"It would be fair if my client's I.D is revealed after the case if he wishes to do so"

"Ha that's if you win this and get anonymity for your criminal robot enterprise, you can't defend them all".

Samuel tries to enquire as to how evidence of his client's I.D was obtained by Robert? Since only he and the client should know but Samuel can't prove there's any illegal way the evidence was obtained but the judge does press Robert for evidence that it was obtained legally to which he can't prove thus the I.D of Kingsley is omitted giving Samuel a big advantage in his case. How could Robert have been so sloppy? Surely he thought of this. Sam is bemused.

Robert puts forward his witnesses and experts there's no surprise or need for Sam to ask questions. Sam mentions to the judge he has been in contact with a scientist called James Ryan and is currently unable to provide exact details of how he is relevant to the case
"Alright Mr.Hughes"
"Feel free to call me Sam please your honour we are not in court yet"
"I think we will keep things professional here Mr.Hughes, I need to be informed as soon as you know what this scientist is seeking to come and prove"
I can't have any surprises
"I know you're not like some of these cowboy lawyers shooting from the hip"
He looks over at Robert who has a smirk on his face.

"Yes your honour, I'm curious myself"
Robert is a bit off guard
"Oh come on how can we have a surprise like this I need time to prepare and rebut"
Making a lunging pose as if sword fighting.
"Mr.Chowe I'll have none of your theatrics here or in my court! Do you hear me?"
"Yes of course your honour".

Opening statements (day 1 of the case)
The judge walks in, with his long black robes Robert, Samuel and the rest that are gathered are already standing before him since the court warden said
"All rise for the honourable Judge Douglas".
Addressing the court
"the accused let's call him Mr.Z for now since we are dealing with whether we should know his true identity stands accused today of non-disclosure of his identity for the purpose of purchasing a property"
Kingsley has been sworn in.
"How do you plead?"
Kingsley responds standing next to Samuel
"Innocent, your honour".
"Ok have a seat everyone".
The judge addresses the jury making sure they understand their purpose
"you 12 individuals' ladies and gentleman have been asked today to decide upon whether Mr.Z should have a right as a pod user to not disclose his identity (who he was before becoming a pod user) for the purposes of purchasing a property".
The case had reached the level of the court due to the fact that Kingsley had gone through most of the property transfer process and was close to securing it until his I.D was found to be fake. In all the years of pods this has not happened because people understood there is no point trying to lie about who you were but Kingsley had tried his luck based on the fact he was trying to escape rivals and start fresh in life.

The prosecution, Robert steps forward and states his case using the world population,
"Your honour if humans are to continue using pods what is going to happen with a world population steadily increasing? Due to less deaths with a large portion of people opting for pods. This places a huge demand on housing, food supply and natural resources".

Robert then argued religion if there was a trick left unused he wasn't going to leave it behind the only thing not used by him is the kitchen sink
"Most religions speak of a judgement after death and pods are removing this element a very vital element for the living to know that if a person has done bad or good they shall be judged just like how this client is being judged and there shall be a sentence passed based on their actions"

Waving his finger up and down at Kingsley like he was telling off a naughty child, Kingsley smirks
"What happens when a family member has someone killed by a pod-user? A pod user who for whatever reason should be 6ft under, but due to technology is now alive in a pod and has caused this tragedy"

Next Robert took the moral high ground
"What about I ask you ladies and gentlemen of the jury a pod-user knowing things about a person they knew and not disclosing who they were and having the appearance of someone else, do humans really control the pod?".

His calm pacing back and forth trying to get the jury on his side almost rhythmic
"I am here on behalf of humanity"

The defence Samuel is called and argues his client is entitled to his privacy and wanting to start a new life and not wanting to be judged based on his previous escapades and if Robert stands with RealLife and believes pods shouldn't exist? Robert rebuts this as only he can with humour
"They should exist but we should know who is actually inside these things"

Smirking
"You know I could be looking at my 73 year old grandma in a pod that looks 25 on the outside hitting on me?"

The jury chuckle he winks at them
"Some weird things could take place your honour and that's what I am trying to prevent".

The judge intercedes
"Well we know there are limitations in place to prevent pod users going into a pod that is too young looking, we've had people die at 80 and come back in a 25 year old body that's the youngest any pod can look and they all have to be adults, no teenagers no kids"

Sam places his hand on Kingsley's shoulder before walking in front of the jury
"My client has tried to change his life your honour. You know his past and I cannot disclose it to the jury because that might give weight to a biased opinion but he is a reformed character and in being this new character wished to purchase a property away from this current location to move on with his life and escape all bad associations and his previous life".

The TV flicks off James Ryan has watched the trial on African TV with interest his ticket is already booked for a flight after speaking with Sam about some evidence he might have to help with the case.

Witness testimony (day 2)

When called upon by Sam, James Ryan states

" The Nano-bots and AI use a sophisticated unique language different to that of Java or other known internet languages". The bots can and will perform tasks using this language, presumably so the bots cannot be commanded by any outsiders but also so no wrong information or viruses can go back to Bertha".

James Ryan shows the Wi-Fi signals of bots and their behaviour change as well as their code during and after the signal on a screen to the court. It shows the Nano bots up close with the Wi-Fi signal when active and when off. There is a noticeable difference in their activity which explained by James Ryan showing the results of what their code says their main objective is when the Wi-Fi is off and when on. When on, the bots complete sophisticated tasks and can adapt to what the pod user is doing and learn fast but when off they have their basic acquired skills and cannot learn or adapt and, in some instances, as reported by various users it causes the user to freeze or pause until sufficient data or updates are received.

The prosecution cross examines Kingsley
The defence cross examines Dr's from Burls on how they operate and do they deviate from orders for money to allow criminals to go in different pods? To which they all state no, who would implicate themselves and face prosecution? Even under oath.

James Ryan comes forward that supports the theory that Nano bots can control humans. This was thought to be untrue until the scientist shows experiments conducted on birds that fly to countries they had never flown before at the wrong time of year, proving that their natural instinct that they have had for years to fly to the same locations at the right time of year to avoid cold is somehow either disrupted or overridden. The scientist states he believes Nano bots are within everyone the only reason he has escaped and people in the village he is working in (Africa) is due to lack of Wi-Fi that disrupts Nano bot behaviour because no signal is being received so they operate with simply their prime objectives.

So Robert questions
"Well since you're here now in America are Nano bots in you and controlling you?"
James R. responds I have a device on me that disrupts Wi-Fi signals up to 2 metres within my range I didn't want anything influencing my views and opinions, it is safe to any pod users around because it doesn't penetrate through a pod just human flesh".

A call comes in from Vanessa to Sam during a trial break
"Sam"
"Yeah! What is it? Your voice sounds shaky"
He knows this is how she sounds before breaking down and crying.
"Don't panic but… well they want me to go in hospital asap"
"Ok, that's a bit out of the blue have they said what the problem is? And if it is treatable?"
"No not much I'll know more when I go".

Sam is stressed running his fingers through his hair

"Alright let me finish up here and I'll come straight away text me the ward"

Closing arguments (day 3) brief statement and summarising.

Judge addresses jurors explaining the crime the defendant is charged with and reminds the jury it has to be "beyond reasonable doubt" before they can convict. The jury go to discuss the case in a small back room before re-appearing.

Verdict

The foreman reads out the statement handed to him from the jury

"We the jury find unanimously the defendant x is not guilty of I.D fraud for the purposes of benefiting solely for gain but gets a minimised sentence based on guilty plea to a ten-month suspended sentence and fine of $1,000".

A few shouts of

"yyyeesss"

And claps are heard Kingsley hugs Sam passionately patting him on his right back shoulder. Sam and Kingsley have left the court and are in a side room with changing facilities and are discussing how things went. Kingsley is changing from his suit into something more comfortable a blue jeans and t-shirt when Robert enters. The smile that was on Sam's face has left

"what is it Robert?"

"I just wanted to congratulate you Sam for a second I thought you wasn't going to pull it off and I would have to somehow jeopardise my case to save Kingsley"

Sam has a puzzled look on his face he knew Robert was a joker and crazy at the best of times, Robert paces over to Kingsley fast. Sam panics that Robert might be upset and looking to confront Kingsley in some way which would not be good for Robert's health.

"hey my man"

Kingsley stands up straight from tying his trainers and Robert embraces him with a one-armed clasping of hands and pat from the other hand on the shoulder.

"Robert this isn't the way I wanted to tell him!"

"Tell me what?"

Sam's face is frowned partly because of what's just happened but also because he needs to meet Vee.

"Look Sam the long and short of it is I had faith that you can do the job but I had paid Robert just to ensure everything went smooth and there was nothing too damaging against me"

Sam shouts slamming his fist into one of the lockers denting it

"You did what?"

"Come on, you're a great lawyer but I can't rely on that alone"

Kingsley walks to the door to leave

"look thank you for all your help Sam I know you have to rush off otherwise I would buy you a drink don't be mad about it, it's just business"

Offering his hand for Sam to shake. It takes Sam longer than it should to stretch his hand out in response but he knows who he's dealing with, he is expendable to Kingsley now. Reluctantly he shakes his hand. Looking first at Sam then Robert, Kingsley smiles

"See you guys don't fight!"

Kingsley exits the room. Sam still believing Kingsley is a good guy says at least his client can live a normal life now

Robert shakes his head sideways

"these guys don't change, he's paying me and probably the judge"

he walks towards a locker to open it, laughing smugly

"I got bills to pay Sam, even when I lose I win!"

After opening it and removing something from a bag he places an expensive looking cigar in Sam's front blazer pocket tapping it with his hand as if to ensure it is in. Sam already had a slight dislike for Robert due to his arrogance and joking around but this infuriated him to think he didn't genuinely win and that Kingsley had played possum all along when asking questions about the case and if they could win when all along he knew he had the upper hand and wasn't really threatened with jail in any way.

END

Chapter 16 Bar Crawl

It is night time Samuel is drinking in a half decent bar after winning his court case for Kingsley. It is a mixture of trying to celebrate and drown his sorrows at the same time, after finding out Vee had died due to organ failure. Vanessa has always been against re-birth so he is arguing with the bar tender about having another drink he just can't comprehend it. The kids haven't been told and are being looked after by Julie.
"Just one more I can handle my drink!"
Banging his fist against the bar causing a small bowl of peanuts to jump whilst arguing why his wife couldn't give Re-birth a try
"She's so against it, I can't understand why?"
A few minutes later a woman walks in calmly approaching the bar. She has looked around to see who's there and talks to Sam whilst his head is downwards against the bar sobbing. Sam doesn't look up but merely answers her questions. She orders a drink of Baileys and sits on the seat next to him, he mutters
"That was my wife's favourite drink"
"Really, you say was? What happened to her?"
He explains of her organ failure as if it seemingly stemmed from no-where, the warning signs were there from the stomach cramps but she probably ignored it for a while trying to put her duty to her family first as she always did. This fact compiled with Roberts words
Even when I lose I win

Is irritating him and swirling around his head much like the alcohol.

Vanessa's built up resentment finally comes out she finds herself almost mimicking her mother's words and hand gestures to explain the pain of

"Having to give birth before my parts were no good like a product on a shelf waiting to expire".

Sam is bewildered not knowing what she is on about this supposed stranger has started talking about something totally random to him and he thought he had issues.

The conversation continues between them as they are the last two in the bar.

Samuel wakes up in the morning in his bed he goes to make breakfast searching for the hangover cure of a fried breakfast. On the breakfast bar he sees his wife's wedding ring, standing out against the white. He thought the ring would be with her when she was ready for burial. He rushes to the bar to ask the bar tender about the woman he was talking to last night and asks for footage from the camera in the bar. He's shown a video the woman's face is obscured he can only see her long hair a different colour to that of his wife's and the shape of her. Asking the bar tender Mitch have you seen this woman before?

"No"

He answers.

"She just asked me to tell you a weird message she said everything is alright now you was right about being Re-Born, please look after yourself and the kids and she ordered a cab and took you home". Samuel responds "how did she get me in a cab?"

"I helped her, you were out on your feet I thought you got lucky and she was taking you to her place".

"I got to find her"

Samuel scrambles to his feet, he pauses, his hand making the motion back and forth like he was about to run. Mick shouts

"Sam, Sam, you alright? you look like you're a pod mate paused and glitching back and forth hahaha"

It's been a few seconds Mick realises this isn't right jumps over the bar with two feet and his hands pressed down on the surface of the bar and assesses Samuel

"for fuck sake Sam you couldn't tell anyone no wonder you were fighting for that prick you're one of them, you're a bloody pod! "

He drags Samuel off behind the bar and plugs him in to charge.

END

Chapter 17 Bertha's conflict

During the trial Real-Life has implemented their plan to attack Bertha with a virus it sounds easy but it is a highly sophisticated piece of code uploaded through presumed pod users who support R.L with info going back to Bertha infecting her allowing pod users to realise they hadn't necessarily been themselves when choosing a different body after taking in the nano – bots before and then after death. There will be a specific time for them to attack when an EMP (Electro Magnetic Pulse) is used to take down Bertha's shield they can do this by tracking her radioactive signal, which is distinctive to all electronic devices but in this case, it is not such a hidden fact what the radioactive signal is for A.I due to safety protocols to ensure human safety.

What was the motivation on behalf of the bots or Bertha for spreading outside of pods? Does it give the bots or Bertha more freedom to start a fresh life rather than continue someone else's previous life? Who knows.

The A.I code that affected Bertha is traceable to the Nevada dessert i.e. area 51. The tech wiz Samuel and Kingsley were using couldn't get results but an underground hacker came forward to offer his services in return for being cleared of going to trial for previous criminal activity involving hacking. He helps to locate the signal and thus where the Nano-bots and Bertha had problems. They question if area 51 had something to do with it could they be prepping pods for alien use so aliens can walk amongst humans without any issues. It would explain why a few pods have been found without brains and spines but a set of nerves and a slime like substance inside. Often when pods were found like this it was just dismissed as a major malfunction that occurred that might have fried the brain and spine inside the pod but this isn't the case.

After looking through the A.I code, backup and files it is discovered Bertha hid the fact that it controls the Nano bots remotely with updates. People always thought the bots were programed to just operate inside the body and had programed jobs but signals were being sent to Bertha from the bots and back.

Many pod users come forward after the Nano-bots A.I connection is shut down they want to change to the pod that resembled their former self re-uniting family members across the world. The law is now seeking to find out if nano-bots are indeed affecting everyday humans and thus breaching human rights and this could lead to bigger action against the pod companies with tighter regulations imposed and stop the production of pods altogether.

END

Chapter 18 Face to Face once more

Sam is in a rage that Vanessa has used the process of being Re-Born without wanting to be with him and taking on a new form. Pacing back and forth it runs through his head how Kingsley partly lied about wanting to be legitimate and didn't disclose to Sam that he knew Vanessa. Enraged he seeks Kingsley out with a hand gun and silencer taken from his home safe, he may be the son of a major criminal and has chosen a different path but he always kept in mind his dad's past could come back to haunt him and ensured he had protection for any such event.

Sam is speaking to his kids before leaving the kids with Julie to pursue Kingsley and Vanessa.

"Dexter, Sarah, you're going to spend some time with nana Julie whilst I try and find out how true all this stuff on the news is about Nano-bots controlling people, making them choose different pods to the one's resembling themselves"

Dexter interrupts

"Why's that so important dad?"

Julie clears her throat

"Urrrgghhh what about Kingsley? You know he's dangerous!"

Sam smirks putting his hands behind his back clasped as if to show innocence

"What about him?"

"He only partly lied to you; it must be hard for him to escape that life. Don't get caught up in a world that's not yours".

Samuel gives Julie a peck on the cheek before stepping back through the kids and kissing them. He puts his left hand on Dexter's right shoulder looking down on his face as if to reassure him his actions would either bring their mother back or in some way get Kingsley back for his deception. It is brief but Dexter nods as if he understands, Sarah standing next to Dexter has her arms outstretched for a hug, which he gives her she was always more affectionate than Dexter.

The kids don't know about their mum possibly being in a pod they thought she was so against it especially with her religious belief but Julie knows and nods standing behind the children a hand placed on each childs' shoulder.

Sam closes the front door to his home looking back knowing the decision he is making to confront Kingsley after the trial is a dangerous one, especially since he has taken a gun with him.

As he approaches the mansion he can see Kingsley has a few goons outside guarding the doors, two to be exact but there could be one patrolling the grounds. Guarded or not this doesn't matter for now, his mission is to confront Kingsley get the information on Vanessa's whereabouts and leave whether that's with Kingsley alive or not he hasn't decided as if he has much choice on this issue. Sam knows only someone with connections can help Vee escape without a trace, pod or no pod, Sam has his connections through being in the law and could normally pull up info on people or activity if not by his own methods he could through using someone else.

After buzzing to get through the gates and giving his name to a goon to verify himself with Kingsley the gate beeps and swings open he approaches the door where the two other gang members are standing. One steps forward to pat him down as expected he has the silencer positioned very close to his groin hoping through not wanting to look homosexual the guard will just do a quick pat and miss the gun. He has missed it and Sam is allowed to enter the goon with a deep voice advises him
    "Straight ahead there's a door, between the staircase that winds up on the left and right"
As he enters Kingsley is in a night robe sitting on a swivel leather chair behind a desk casually with no one else in sight alone in a room, seems like the perfect chance for him a bit too perfect.

As if Kingsley knows Sam's intent must be Vanessa's whereabouts he explains when he discussed his identity for buying the property and gave over documents he knew his enemies would return so he couldn't escape his old life and needed protection from his gang. Keeping his gang required him to continue various activities as he couldn't be seen to be doing nothing, this would make him seem soft or out of step where his enemies could take over or if not that he could be challenged internally from his own people. Gary was doing a good job in his absence but didn't command the same respect from other gangs and although he couldn't let other gangs know he was alive he still had to get involved a bit more than he wanted to ensure his gang and area didn't crumble and get taken over.

Sam is standing listening intently weighing up what his actions should be, he hasn't moved from his stance in front of the desk. After a few minutes of listening to Kingsley talk about himself and his predicament he knows Kingsley has avoided talk of his wife, so he jumps in to cut him off mid-sentence.

"What can you tell me about Vanessa's whereabouts? Is she even in the country?"

"She is but doesn't wish to be contacted by you, she wanted to start fresh and I respected that and told her I would not disclose her location"

"You understand we have kids that are just abandoned now?"

"Yes I do I suggested she take the kids but she said it would damage you too much and the lifestyle she wants to pursue would be easier without kids and she knew she could trust you to raise them correctly"

"So that's it after how many years of marriage? She gets to disappear and destroy everything we had to pursue a career?"

"Did you even notice her decline Sam?"

Sam's fists are clenching he is not liking what he's hearing

"What do you mean?"

"In the later stages Sam, you didn't realise she became unclean, unkept, didn't wash her hair man come on! She was frail, who do you think kept her going financially paid for doctor appointments and pills you probably didn't even know about"

Sam's lost for words and shouts

"I, I was busy helping you!"

Shots are fired "Pew, Pew"...

END

Chapter 19 Sam's Dialogue

So I spend most of my days now looking for my Vanessa. I say "my" but it is Sam's really. I know you're confused right? When Sam died he wanted to be re-born he told me if anything goes wrong I should take action to ensure he was replaced with a replica pod and use any means necessary to ensure the family never knew any different and thought it was his spine and brain inside the pod, why would they think otherwise? That ten hour period between death and being re-born I mentioned earlier is important! when the doctors got to Sam it took them too long they were unsure of the time period that had passed and acted quickly but unfortunately it was too little too late.

So who is in Sam's replica pod? Me, his long-term friend Eddie Roberts, Sam left me all his notes on phrases and main events of his life, memories with Vanessa and the kids and he always spoke to me about these things so when he died it seemed no one else could do a better job. I spoke with his father when he was alive and he approved everything and saw to it I was "available" so to speak with the help of his loyal men. They made it a quick and pain free process I'm sure with their expertise they could have made it very painful but this was a job for their boss so their heads were on the line.

Why would someone give such as sacrifice? I had nothing going on for me really, Sam's life I admired for years he had everything a family, wealth, a great career I was just the friend with the 9-5 job little pay no family of my own and family that were blood but treated me like a black sheep. As Sam I have it all a chance to be fresh and start again with loving kids that adore me and I am fulfilled and can achieve so much more as Sam.

The government now want to find out who is responsible for the problems faced by Bertha and to know what effect this can have on humans in general. They now start to question whether pod users can be in politics whilst having major decisions over humans and whether they can be in other prominent high-profile jobs because they might not be themselves and could be controlled in some manor by Nano-bots or Bertha.

It is being suggested that individuals who choose to come back in a different pod body form to what they were in whilst alive have their memory erased, so there is no recollection of who they were and they cannot have information on people they used to know whilst not disclosing their former self.

END

Printed in Great Britain
by Amazon